# VIETNAM
## - Port Townsend Bay

# VIETNAM
# - Port Townsend Bay

Calmar Austin McCune

Copyright © 2025 by Calmar Austin McCune.

Library of Congress Control Number: 2025918394
ISBN: Hardcover 979-8-3694-5247-9
Softcover 979-8-3694-5246-2
eBook 979-8-3694-5245-5

All rights reserved. No part of this book may be reproduced or transmitted in any form or by any means, electronic or mechanical, including photocopying, recording, or by any information storage and retrieval system, without permission in writing from the copyright owner.

This is a work of fiction. Names, characters, places and incidents either are the product of the author's imagination or are used fictitiously, and any resemblance to any actual persons, living or dead, events, or locales is entirely coincidental.

Any people depicted in stock imagery provided by Getty Images are models, and such images are being used for illustrative purposes only.
Certain stock imagery © Getty Images.

Print information available on the last page.

Rev. date: 08/19/2025

To order additional copies of this book, contact:
Xlibris
844-714-8691
www.Xlibris.com
Orders@Xlibris.com
868475

"Ticket Desk 22 to Tower," spoken in the language of Vietnam.

"Tower, here."

"We have a long line for Flight 388 leaving Hanoi for Ho Chin Min City. Could you please delay departure so we can get all on board?"

"Roger. Will do."

Weary, the ticket taker glanced up at the long line. He noticed a lovely woman at the end of the line.

"Hey, Minh, look at the lady at the end of the line. Chinese women are so lovely."

Minh raised his head and said, "She is gorgeous. She is not Chinese. She is Vietnamese."

When her turn came, the lady presented no ticket. "Tell me, please, is Flight Triple Zero due?"

Glancing at the large overhead electronic arrival panel, the ticket taker replied, "There is no Flight Triple Zero."

"Please," she said, "ask Tower."

"Desk 22 to Tower."

"Yes."

"Do we have an incoming Flight Triple Zero?"

"Tower back, yes, it is on radar, about five miles out."

"Counter to Tower, why is Flight Triple Zero coming here?"

"Tower back. Not certain. Plane, a Boeing 747, privately owned and has government clearance. I can see it now. Reportedly, plane owned by the wealthiest person in Vietnam. Tower out."

The ticket taker turned to the woman and told her Flight Triple Zero was due shortly. "Are you boarding?"

"Yes."

"Are you a flight nurse?"

"No, I am an in-flight doctor."

"Where did you go to medical school?"

"I have a medical degree from Harvard in the United States and an advanced degree from the Royal London Institute of Surgery."

"As a surgeon, do you have a specialty?"

"Yes, facial reconstruction."

"Cosmetic?"

"No, trauma, like where a plane crashes and the pilot's jaw is in ten pieces and needs to be reconstructed. From time to time, I take jobs escorting ailing wealthy people."

From a window, she watched the plane approach. For years, she had admired the Boeing 747. She guessed that excessive fuel consumption had caused the Boeing 747 to lose popularity. She listened to the reverse thrusters and watched as the plane slowly rolled forward. A truck stopped next to the plane and extended its ladder up to a door on the main deck of the plane. Shortly, a door opened, and the captain appeared and descended the steps. He walked into the airport, met Dr. Thu, and escorted her to the plane.

"Why no windows along the side of the plane?" she asked. "This plane is a cargo plane. It is designed to carry freight or many people. There are no seats. Passengers simply sit on the floor and hold a rope secured to the deck. The front of the plane is hinged so it can be lifted up to allow containers to be loaded."

"How can one person afford this plane?"

The captain replied, "He is a successful businessman and can easily afford the costs. Actually, the plane is on call to the government. Maintenance and staffing are done by the government."

"Why?"

"From time to time, the government may need to move hundreds of flood victims. It may need to transport many troops. When government leaders need to travel to other countries, seats and rooms are temporarily installed, and then the plane makes the leaders look good when they arrive."

Dr. Thu looked around. "I understand I am helping a Mr. Dexter Rowell. Who is he?"

## Vietnam - Port Townsend Bay

"He is an old man. His doctors say he has two weeks to live. He is in the first room aft to your left. You will have plenty of time to get to know him. He is strapped to a bed."

"What is his sickness?"

"I do not know. When you enter his room, you will notice a couch alongside the bed. That is for you to sit and to sleep on. When requested, you will be sure that Mr. Rowell and you are strapped. The bed and the couch are bolted to the floor. His room has an adjoining bathroom on one side and a medical supply room on the other. The rooms are all temporary and are removed when the plane hauls cargo. Good to have you on board. We will take off in ten minutes."

"Thank you."

The captain turned and ascended the steps to the top deck. Just as he left, the copilot appeared. He handed the doctor a headset that would cover one ear and asked that she wear it during the flight.

She asked him, "What is the flight plan?"

He answered, "We refuel in Honolulu and fly on to Paine Field near Everett, Washington, United States.

"Why there?"

"Mr. Rowell grew up in that region, and now he wishes to go home."

A couch next to a bed was all she saw when she opened the door. The bed looked empty.

When she walked closer, she realized a small person was on the bed, asleep. Wide cotton straps crossed the bed to hold the sleeper in place. One strap ran across just below his shoulders. A second strap lay across his hips. A third strap ran from one side of the bed over his ankles to the other side. Upon sitting down, she leaned forward to touch Mr. Rowell's neck.

*He has a pulse*, she thought to herself. He slept. She sat.

A weighted truck on the tarmac nudged the front of the 747 and pushed it backward several hundred feet, then pivoted it 180 degrees so the plane faced away from the airport. Four engines accelerated to move enough air to push the plane forward along an access lane until the plane turned and faced down the runway.

On her earphone, the doctor heard the captain say, "Ready for takeoff."

The engines roared, the plane sort of jiggled and then moved slowly, then fast, until, at a ground speed of eighty-six miles an hour, it lifted off. The floor, the bed, and the couch remained at an angle until the plane leveled off at thirty-eight thousand feet.

When she glanced at Mr. Rowell, she saw he was looking at her. "Hello," she said. "How are you?"

"I am fine, just weak. How does one feel when doctors say he has two weeks to live? You know doctors exaggerate. That means I have one week to live."

"Would you like the bed adjusted so you can sit up?"

"Yes."

She examined an electrical panel, pushed a button, and slowly the bed changed from a flat platform to create an inclining back wall. She loosened the straps and gently lifted Mr. Rowell into a sitting position. She placed two pillows under his knees.

"Why are you traveling?"

"Why am I traveling?"

"Yes, why?"

"Maybe I am slightly mentally ill."

"How's that?"

"Melancholy. Often, I look back in time, and I become nostalgic about memories of the past, especially of my parents. They passed on years ago, but even now, my mind teases me into believing my mom and dad are still alive, waiting for me around the next corner."

"You had good parents?"

"Yes, the best. My mind plays tricks. For example, a person may know he should not eat too much or should not drink alcohol, but he still gorges on food or binges on alcohol. The part of the brain that commands our thinking is aware that we are doing the wrong thing but is helpless. In my case, I know my parents have been dead for years, but some unbalanced part of my thinking tells me each parent is still alive and waiting for me. So I go into a state of euphoria, knowing we will soon be together, and then I enter a mental condition of severe depression. It is a nasty cycle I cannot avoid. I decided to spend my last days of life where I once was with my parents."

"Where?"

"A small community northwest of Seattle, Washington. It is a lovely place and is called Port Townsend. Years ago, sailing ships coming off the ocean could tack up wind, back and forth, across what is now called the Strait of Juan De Fuca, like twenty-five miles in width, but farther east, when the waterways narrowed, the ships could tack no more, and some set down anchors at what is now called Port Townsend Bay. With the ships anchored there, the shoreline developed into a town, and huge wharves were built, and wealthy people came to Port Townsend hoping to get richer. And in the process, many Victorian buildings and houses were constructed. My mother inherited a building downtown. I was born there. The bricks in the three-story building were made in Port Townsend. We lived on the top floor, and I played on the roof. The building was intended to be a hotel, but as the economy staggered, it became a brothel. Later, rooms were rented as office space to attorneys and to a credit bureau. From the building, I could walk to school. The classes were small, and the teachers were helpful and friendly.

"As a kid, when I played on the beaches, I would hold a rock in each hand and then toss one rock into the air over the water, and with the other hand, I would toss the rock in an attempt to intercept the first rock. Over time, I became good at hitting the rock. When I was in high school, somehow the football coach learned of my rock-tossing skill. He persuaded me to be on the football team, and I became the quarterback even though I was very small. The coach taught me how to avoid injury. He cautioned that if I were about to be tackled, to simply fall down.

"This game is not worth the injury," he explained. So there I was, leading a football team. For my part, when giving instructions in the huddle, I ignored complex play patterns and simply said, 'Right field,' or 'middle field,' or 'left field,' and then I sort of blindly tossed the football in the suggested direction. Although there were many interceptions, the coach did not seem to mind. Having a losing team was OK with him."

"Do you remember his name?"

"Don Rosbach. He was also a school principal. So, for me, for sure, I am deceiving myself by returning home. No one will know me. My parents and childhood friends will not reappear. How about you? What is your background?"

"I was born in a small village in Vietnam. At the time, there were no roads, just paths from village to village. Everyone was poor, but no one cared for that was our way of life. My parents managed a forest of mulberry trees. They sold or traded the leaves to other villagers who used the leaves to feed silkworms. People in other villages traded for the silkworm cocoons, and then they extracted the silk fiber, twisted it into a fiber, and made silk fabric. My parents also raised water buffalo. Instead of pet dogs or cats, I grew up with massive pet water buffalo."

"Did you run risks of injury?"

"No, unlike the American buffalo or the South African bison, the buffalo in Vietnam were docile. As kids, we would sit and play on top of them. On hot days when we rode a water buffalo, it would walk into a canal and go underwater, and we had to swim to shore."

"Why did it go into the canal?"

"To cool off and to get rid of bugs that were biting its skin."

Mr. Rowell looked distressed. "Look, I need to use the bathroom, but I may be too weak to get there."

"No problem, I can help."

Once he was on the toilet, she left and closed the door. In a few minutes, she heard an odd sound, so she went and opened the bathroom door. Mr. Rowell was on the floor.

He had slid off the toilet. She lifted him and carried him to the bed.

"You OK?"

"Yes, I think so. Slipped off the toilet."

"Captain to in-flight doctor."

"Yes."

"We have a tropical cyclone ahead and a bit to the south. Please secure Mr. Rowell and buckle up. We are turning north about two hundred miles but may still feel the storm."

"OK, we are secure."

The plane dropped its left wing and commenced a gradual turn. Two hundred miles later, it dropped its right wing and continued on a new course to Hawaii. The outward edges of the storm buffeted the plane, causing it to abruptly rise and lower, again and again, but the size and strength of the plane allowed for easy passage.

"What do you eat?"

"Mostly fortified chocolate milk, sometimes rice mashed with sweet potato."

"Fortified by what?"

"Vegetable-sourced protein."

"There is a stash in a small refrigerator in the medical supply room. We can have a party."

She entered the side room, opened the refrigerator, and saw about thirty plastic bottles of chocolate milk. She took one for herself and one for Mr. Rowell. He needed a bendable straw, and she found one.

"Cheers," he exclaimed.

"Cheers," she replied.

Soon, there was a knock on the door, and the captain slowly opened the door and entered. After sitting on the couch, he declined the offer of a bottle of chocolate milk. He glanced at Mr. Rowell to be certain he was secure.

"When we reach Honolulu, there will be a four-hour stopover. You may want to look about."

"No. Thanks. My job is to stay close to Mr. Rowell. I have been to Oahu before and have seen much of it."

The captain probed, "What part of the island interested you?"

She answered, "Three areas: The western edge called Kaena Point, where albatrosses nest; the eastern edge called Makapuu, and the top of a volcano called Koko Head. At Makapuu, from the parking lot, I would walk to a rock formation called Pele's Chair, and then I would walk counterclockwise around it and walk on a lava bench toward the east. The walk is dangerous, and one must go at low tide. Along the way is a huge tidal pool and a cave, and then one comes to several tide pools in which one can rest. Nearby one hears explosive sounds, like a steam-engine railroad going uphill. There is a horizontal lava tube there, and when ocean waves enter the tunnel, pressure builds up and spray is forced upward to the surface, and a roaring sound is made. Locals call it the Devil's Nostrils. I also like just staring at Diamond Head Volcano."

"How is Mr. Rowell?"

"His pulse is OK. As you can see, he has fallen asleep again. Why does Mr. Rowell own such a large plane?"

The captain glanced at Mr. Rowell to be certain he slept. He explained, "He uses the plane as a cargo plane to transport his products. In fact, the plane is on call to the government. It is maintained and manned by government employees."

"Why?"

Dr. Thu asked, "What is his business?

"I should not gossip. This is a long flight. You have plenty to ask Mr. Rowell." He left.

Mr. Rowell, upon opening his eyes, said, "Hello again."

"How are you?" she asked.

"No pain, but I am very weak. My muscles are not very responsive and often cramp."

"Why are you so weak?"

He turned his head and looked directly at her. "Stenosis of the aortic valve—that is what the doctors say. Do you know about it?"

"Yes, my father passed on because of it."

"Recently?"

"Four years ago."

Mr. Rowell went on: "Surgery is possible, sewing into me the coronary valve of a barnyard animal. I do not want to be cut open. I am old. It is time for my life to end."

"You have decided to go on this long journey, why?"

"I seem to think a lot of the town where I grew up. The people I knew there, the schools, my parents—they all seem to possess my attention. It is true that Vietnam is my home, and I am grateful for that, but at the same time, I would be grateful to see the place where I spent my youth. As I may have mentioned, often, I daydream that my parents are still alive, waiting for me. I am sort of haunted by a vision of a reunion. As I am going to die, I just as well pass on in Port Townsend."

Once more, there was a knock on the door and this time the cocaptain entered.

"Reportedly, we are in a traffic lane where we are not supposed to be, so in a few minutes, we will again be banking north. The tower at Honolulu has ordered a change in our flight plan. He stepped back and left.

In a few minutes, the plane again dropped its left wing and headed north and then, after twenty minutes, changed direction to reach Honolulu.

Mr. Rowell kept talking: "You might say that just as a duck is imprinted to its mother, I am imprinted to my parents. I think of them often and miss each dearly."

"Have you stayed in touch with friends from Port Townsend?"

"I did, but slowly, correspondence petered off. Most of my classmates have passed on."

"Did you have a classmate who was a close friend?"

"Yes, I spent a lot of time at the home of Tom Tucker. His father was a rockhound and had lapidary machines in his garage. He encouraged the two of us to take his metal detector and to walk along the foot of bluffs to try to find gold nuggets that had eroded off the face of the cliffs."

"Find anything?"

"No, but over the years, I did realize Tom and I were happy simply to have the hope of finding gold, as though the sense of hope was itself golden. We did find one mastodon rib. It was too heavy to move, and we knew it would break apart once fully exposed to air. We simply left a note with directions at the local museum."

Dr. Thu noticed Mr. Rowell's skin was turning purple. She grabbed an oxygen tank from the medical supply room, attached a tube and breathing mask, and placed it over Mr. Rowell.

"In-flight doctor to captain."

"Yes."

"Mr. Rowell is temporarily on oxygen. I wonder if you can take the plane down a bit so I might then be able to remove the mask?"

"I'll get clearance from Honolulu. We will then descend to sixteen thousand feet."

"Thank you."

"Captain back. What is the problem?"

"His skin has turned purple."

"Why?"

"I do not know for certain. Hard to tell. My guess is that his aortic valve cannot attain a full aperture, thereby his red blood cells remain depleted of needed oxygen."

"What causes the valve problem?"

"Teeth."

"Teeth?"

"Yes, if a person fails to keep teeth brushed and clean, a bacterial film will form around the teeth, sometimes called plaque. From there, the bacteria will slip into the bloodstream and float about until it can find a place to settle, which happens to be the plates of the aortic valve. Think of it as barnacles growing, forming a crusty surface that prevents the valve from fully opening. Oxygen is denied, and weakness and death follow."

The captain said, "I never get my teeth cleaned. Am I doomed to an early death?"

"Maybe," the doctor replied, "just get your teeth cleaned four times a year."

Mr. Rowell awakened. He glanced over at Dr. Thu and saw she was looking at a laptop.

"What are you watching?"

"I am reviewing a new patient. Yesterday, she went through a car windshield, and now her nose is cut off and her jaw is broken in three places. Her face is swollen now. In a week, I may be able to operate."

"What will you do?"

"Rebuild her face. I can graft bone and skin and use titanium braces."

"Have you done this before?"

"Not exactly. Each case is different. Her body will want to heal, and she will be unconscious while I work on her."

"Will her face dry out before the operation?"

"No. She is in a special hospital, and the special fluids are brushed and sprayed on her face."

"Do you fret and worry about such an operation?"

"No. In England, I was well taught. We practiced hundreds of times over dead bodies. Then we spent a year assisting real surgeons. We were almost constantly on call. In the final year, we performed surgeries under school supervision."

"Will you meet the new patient?"

"Probably. It is customary to meet, but sometimes the patient has already been anesthetized."

Mr. Rowell commented, "I will never see you again."

"That is true. Once we arrive at Paine Field, I will rent a car and head for Sea-Tac to catch a plane for Boston."

She asked, "What will you do?"

"Once we land, there will be a driver and an SUV waiting for me to drive me to Port Townsend. Once there, I have rented for three weeks a street-level hotel room that is located downtown near where I grew up."

"Will you be on your own?"

"Yes. I will die there, be cremated there, placed into a shoe box, and, according to directions in my wallet, I will be scattered at low tide on the beach at Fort Worden."

"Did you marry?"

"Yes. A Vietnamese lady. A fine companion for many years. Her lungs became infected with TB, and then the bacteria moved to her spine and then to her brain, and she passed on.

"Children?"

"Yes, three daughters. Each died very young due to malformations caused by Agent Orange."

"Captain to in-flight doctor. Please secure your patient and yourself. We are about to land at Honolulu."

The plane descended to six hundred feet and then seemed to parade by Diamond Head and Waikiki. In a few minutes, it turned back and landed.

"Captain here. Refueling will take one hour, and then we will taxi upwind to a waiting pad, where we can then open all doors for fresh air. We will wait there for approximately three hours."

Later, at the waiting pad, Mr. Rowell commented, "I think I can smell plumeria, can you?"

"Yes. Maybe there is a grove farther upwind."

Once airborne, the 747 continued on at sixteen thousand feet toward Washington State.

"Tell me, Mr. Rowell, how did you come to live in Vietnam?"

"My high school grades were so poor that I knew no college would accept me. I enlisted in the army. Aptitude tests suggested I should study chemistry with the purpose of becoming an expert in explosives. I took many chemistry classes and studied explosives. I was assigned to a base called Dong Zu, which is about twenty miles northeast of Saigon. The base was new and very large. It was in an area called Cu Chi.

"When?"

"March of 1966. I was eighteen."

"What did you do there?"

"Well, as you may know, in parts of Vietnam, military tunnels existed and initially were ignored by the United States Army. Cu Chi base, for example, had about eight miles of tunnels. Instead of having a war where enemies faced off and fought each other, like in WWI, rather, the Vietnamese military simply disappeared underground. In the tunnels were a hospital, ammunition stores, kitchens, and places for hundreds of soldiers to sleep and to be ready to attack Saigon. The base commander realized something had to be done, but he was not certain what. He decided to seek volunteers who could descend into small holes and then move along tunnels. I volunteered and was one of the few accepted. We formed a team of eight people, and we would be called upon to go by helicopter from place to place where tunnels had been discovered.

"Each time I was scared out of my wits, but I went. The tunnels began to be built in the 1940s to avoid being seen by French spotter planes. Later, the tunnels were expanded, from village to village. Then when the North Vietnamese Army became engaged in the south of Vietnam, extensive tunnel work was done. The tunnels could hide, like, five thousand soldiers. Some soldiers stayed underground for many years. The soil was called laterite and was composed of clay and iron. It was so solid that when a tunnel was dug, no shoring was necessary. Villagers—women, children, and old men—turned out to dig the tunnels, bit by bit. They received no pay. By 1966, there were about two hundred miles of tunnels in southern Vietnam. The typical passageway was twenty-four inches wide and thirty inches high. At the tunnel opening and along the tunnels were many booby traps. I had to move slowly through a tunnel, often with my light off. I had a dagger, a gun, and no uniform. We were called tunnel rats. In the tunnels were malarial mosquitoes, venomous snakes, six-inch-long scorpions, fire ants, venomous centipedes, and bats. Often, there was almost no oxygen.

"The soil reminded me of the head of Discovery Bay near Port Townsend, for there the soil is much the same as in Vietnam, and I wondered why. The conclusion I reached is that hundreds of miles upriver, or up-sound, glaciers ground mountains into dust, and the rivers carried the dust away to build up as compact clay soil. At Discovery Bay, the southern shoreline is all clay, and it is covered with holes. When the holes are covered at high tide, white-colored ghost shrimp come out and look for food.

"One day at the army base, I was walking with a friend. We were in the middle of the base, far from its perimeter. Suddenly, a shot rang out, and my friend was fatally shot. Medics came. I ran toward the source of the sound and entered a grove of tall bamboo. To my surprise, in front of me was a trapdoor. When I reported my findings, the base commander directed that the trapdoor be shot through and then removed, and that a large, diesel-powered fan be placed over the hole to force smoke from smoke bombs into the tunnel. In a few minutes, the same smoke reappeared about one hundred yards away at six different places. By the time we entered the tunnels, the Vietnamese soldiers had left. We used dynamite to blow up the tunnels, but we had a suspicion that the tunnels could quickly be rebuilt. Each tunnel was at least four and a half feet below the ground, but some tunnels had eight levels and many trapdoors. To gain more oxygen in the tunnels, the Vietcong would place a rabbit in a cage that had only an open top, and then the cage was pressed against the tunnel ceiling using sticks of bamboo. The rabbit would dig upward and, upon reaching the surface, would create an air hole."

"Were you injured?"

"Almost, several times. One time, crawling in darkness along a tunnel, I came to an overhead trapdoor. When I shifted the trapdoor, someone above dropped down a grenade. I knew I was done for, but the grenade was a dud and did not go off. I shot my revolver up through the trapdoor and then hustled backward. Once out of the tunnel, I tossed two grenades, probably a waste of ammunition, but the discharges may have consumed considerable oxygen. The tunnels were never straight for any distance.

One time, I crawled around a corner and turned on my flashlight, and there was in front of me a soldier staring at me. He aimed his rifle at me and shot. The bullet entered my leg. I shot back, but, losing blood, I had to retreat. The wound became infected, and I spent three months at a military hospital. I returned to continue working as a tunnel rat but was captured."

"Captured?"

"Yes, my squad had been helicoptered to a clearing near the border with Cambodia. Tunnels had been discovered there, and our job was to enter and to somehow deny future use of the tunnels. I was the first of six to enter a tunnel, headfirst, no light on, a black hole. Others followed a few feet behind me. The last person carried a portable telephone that had a wire running back to a person on the surface. Somehow, I got slightly ahead of the others, and I entered a side tunnel and got lost. I was in a passageway about five feet below ground level. I came to a trapdoor; I lifted it and shot down. Nothing happened, so I put the trapdoor to one side, and I squeezed down to a lower level. At that second level, I kept crawling, and I came to a new trapdoor on the floor. I moved the trapdoor and dropped down to a third level.

"There I was, in darkness, alone, too curious or stupid to backtrack. Suddenly, my forward hand touched water. I turned on my flashlight and saw that the tunnel continued underwater. The water looked murky and, on the surface, floated a big scorpion. On the wall ahead, I could see many spiders, each one slowly moving toward the light. The tunnel pools were built to block any poisonous gases that we might use to fill the tunnels. After turning my light off, I lowered myself into the filthy water. I had no idea how long the pool might be, or even if there was an exit. I had to hold my breath long enough to back out if necessary.

"About ten feet on, I resurfaced. As I did so, a light flashed on my face, and someone held a rifle pointing at me and he said in clear English, 'Give me your weapons.'

"I complied."

"Follow me."

"At first he moved backward so he could keep his gun on me. We descended down a trapdoor and then crawled along what would be the fourth level. We crawled for another twenty minutes and then descended down another trapdoor to a fifth level. We arrived at a room that was about five feet high and fifteen feet square. At each wall was a tunnel entry. In the middle of the room, five soldiers sat at a worktable. A dim oil light rested in the middle of the table. My arms were forced behind my back, and I could feel my wrists being tied together. At the time, I did not speak Vietnamese, so I had no idea what the other soldiers said. The one who spoke English looked my way and said, 'You are a prisoner. Do not attempt to escape. Do not talk.' I just sat on the floor off to one side. The air was stale. One soldier maintained a small fire, and I watched him boil rice, and then he grilled several rats. Two soldiers in the dim light played a table game called Go. Hours went by. Nothing happened. The fire was small to conserve fuel and oxygen. The smoke was supposed to go up three different chimneys, but some escaped into the room. The air was hard to breathe. Mosquitoes flitted about."

"Were you scared?"

"Always. Just entering a tunnel got the adrenaline going, the heart pounding. Swimming in darkness in a tunnel pool took more nerve than I ever thought I had. In a way, just sitting with others was comforting, but as a prisoner, I had no idea what they might do with me. While I sat, they ignored me. They gave me small portions of grilled rat, rice, and cups of jasmine tea. I sat there for two days.

"On the third day, my legs were stiff. My back hurt. Looking at the Go board, I noticed a player about to make a wrong move, so I grunted and said, 'No.' They stared at me, and then the soldier who spoke English said, 'You know this game?'

"'Yes.'

"'Why did you say no?'

"'Because there is a better move.'

"'How did you learn this game?'

"'In grade school, a Chinese lady named Shirley Tso volunteered to teach me and my classmates how to play the game.'

"'What move do you recommend?'

"'I cannot show you. My wrists are tied.' The soldiers conferred, and one sat away with a rifle pointed at me. Another approached me and freed my wrists. Then I slid my butt over to the players, and I placed my finger down on the proper square. The person I helped win wanted to play me. We did. I won. Each soldier wanted to play against me, and I beat them all, even on rematches. Suddenly, even though I was an enemy, I was respected. I could see that at the worktable, the soldiers were using ammunition to make booby traps. They received reports from lookouts on the surface as to where bombs had landed that had not exploded. At night, they left the tunnels to look for the duds. One stayed behind to keep an eye on me. Once they found a bomb that had not exploded, they would use a hacksaw to cut open the bomb to extract ammunition, which was placed into plastic sacks. Before dawn, they returned to the tunnels. When they returned, each was dry. They must have used tunnels other than the one that had the water trap. The soldier that spoke English would sometimes chat with me. I learned they had been underground for six months. He explained they had aboveground, hidden in the jungle, patches of papaya, mango, and sweet potato. In addition to the fruit, sometimes, only at night, they would go aboveground and walk to a nearby river, where they could catch fresh water prawns. The rice came from a nearby storage room.

"One night, a large explosion took place on the surface, and I could feel the deep tunnel floor shudder. Two soldiers appeared and then disappeared. Something was wrong. Then" the two soldiers appeared with bloody hands and two plastic bulging sacks."

Dr. Thu interrupted, "So what happened?"

Dexter Rowell continued, "Two soldiers had been working to extract ammunition from a bomb, and the heat from the hacksaw caused the bomb to explode. The bags contained their remains. The soldier who spoke English said, 'Now we must go, many miles, to take the bodies to our home village. We have been here long enough. Most of us have malaria from the tunnel mosquitoes. Can we trust you to cause no trouble?'

"Yes."

"We moved out, crawling and walking bent over, for hours, squeezing through many trapdoors. No tunnel pools. When the tunnel ahead offered many side passageways, the soldier in front cast down phosphorous powder along the tunnel edge floor, and when the second soldier flashed his light on the powder, it glowed, showing the way to the others. In the dark, something touched my shoulders, then flapped across my back. I worried a giant scorpion was upon me. Then it happened three more times. The soldier who spoke English was just behind me, and he said, 'Bats.'

"At one tunnel, we seemed to move faster, and the soldier explained, 'Many fire ants are here.'

"The air changed from being stale to smelling of blood. Ahead, we could hear screaming. We entered and passed through an underground room where surgery was being performed without an anesthetic to saw off a leg. Suddenly, the screaming stopped. The patient had either fainted or passed on. We kept moving. Finally, we surfaced in the middle of a jungle. My wrists were tied again. For miles we walked along a jungle trail. Finally, we came to a small village. Uphill from the village, a large meadow was visible. Beyond the village, I could see flat, broad rice ponds. In the middle of the meadow was a shed used to store lotus leaves as food for water buffalo. The shed had no walls, just corner posts to support a thick palm-leaf-covered roof. The soldiers went to their homes. The one who spoke English led me to the shed in the meadow. He kept my wrists bound, and to the binding rope he tied a second rope that was about thirty feet long, and the end of that rope he tied high up to a corner post where I could not reach it.

"'Do not attempt to escape,' he warned me once more. He left, and I moved to the shade of the shed and stretched out on a pile of grass, and went to sleep. My sleep was interrupted by something warm and wet washing my face. Opening my eyes, I saw a huge tongue going back and forth over my face. I thought I was in danger, but in a moment, I realized I was being licked by a huge water buffalo. Soon the licking stopped, and the large animal lay down about three feet from me and went to sleep. Turned out it was the dominant male in a herd of eight. Days went by. Often, the herd leader would rest near me. Village kids hesitantly appeared to play with the water buffalo. They would sit on it and soothe the animal by scratching under its neck. Slowly, the kids became friendly, and I learned their names and then began to pick up from them different words of the Vietnamese language.

"One day, an old man came across the meadow, and he walked to the dominant water buffalo, and while he talked gently, he tied to each horn a long double-sided sharp knife. When the soldier who spoke English checked on me, I asked him about the knives. He explained that people in other villages nearby had seen a heavy male boar. 'That pig,' he said, 'is the most dangerous animal in the jungle. It will attack for no reason and will not stop fighting until dead. The boar does not eat meat. It eats vegetables. But still it attacks. Should a boar attack our herd, then the dominant male will defend. With the knives, he is better prepared.'

"A few days later, while the water buffalo rested near me, I could look across the meadow, and I noticed the herd circling two young, and I could hear the sound of their bellowing. The animal next to me raised its head, heard the bellowing, and charged off to protect the herd. He stood between the herd and the nearby jungle. Maybe the wind had carried the smell of the pig. Soon, branches near the ground moved. A five-hundred-pound boar appeared. It ran fast across the meadow and charged the dominant water buffalo. The pig had two large tusks. It scooted along on short legs. As it charged, the water buffalo lowered its head and stood still. When the pig was almost upon the water buffalo, the water buffalo placed its head at an angle and charged forward to meet the pig. One knife cut into the belly of the pig, and when the water buffalo lifted its head, the pig was tossed into the air. But even then, the boar commenced to attack a second time. The water buffalo again snagged the pig and sent it airborne. For a third time, the pig began to attack. It was losing blood and strength. It and the bigger animal were covered in bright red blood. The pig was determined. Villagers had heard the bellowing and appeared. One raised a rifle and shot the pig. The water buffalo stood staring at the dead pig and then slowly walked back to the shed and lay down near me and rested. While it lay there, villagers brought water and rags and washed the blood off the water buffalo. Other villagers cut the boar into hunks and then carried the meat away.

"I was told I was supposed to join American prisoners in Cambodia, from where we would walk as a group to a prison at Hanoi.

"'Many will die while walking,' the soldier commented. 'Maybe we will try to keep you here.' The villagers became friendly. A sleeping pad of bamboo was built, so I no longer had to sleep on the ground. Bamboo was transplanted from the jungle to be planted around the shed to hide it. Children appeared one day with an old man who carried a gun. He untied me, and he motioned me to follow the children. One child held a rope attached to a metal ring in the nose of the dominant buffalo. After walking across the meadow, we passed through the jungle and then came to the large rice ponds. The water buffalo was led into the rice pound, and it began to eat fresh lotus leaves. We all waded there, trying to catch burrowing crabs. Then the buffalo and I were returned to the meadow.

"Days passed. I taught English words to the kids, and they shared words in their own language. Sometimes parents visited, bringing different types of fruit and cooked prawns. I remained tied but was sort of accepted, if not adopted, by the villagers. I was given dried meat from the wild boar.

One boy came with his older sister, and I felt attracted to her, but I could not converse because my knowledge of the Vietnamese language was so limited. Her name was Ki Nguyen. Eventually, people in other villages learned about me and told the military. Six uniformed soldiers appeared, and I was taken away to be imprisoned in Cambodia. There, the food was poor, and the conditions were squalid. I was with American and Australian servicemen. In two months, we were assembled and ordered to begin to walk over eight hundred miles toward the north, to Hanoi. Unlike the villagers, the guards were impatient and cruel. If a prisoner was sick and could not walk, he was shot. The food lacked protein. We were weak. Often it rained heavily, and we trudged along in thick mud. All the prisoners sustained skin sores. Many suffered from malaria. The walk took four months. Many who started did not survive. As we walked, we were ordered to remain silent. I could eavesdrop on the guards talking, and slowly I learned more words and phrases of their language. After three months of walking, I could understand much of what the guards chatted about. The prison in Hanoi was fairly peaceful, but unpleasant. At the end of the war, I was released and transported back to the United States. My parents were happy to see me. Some of my school chums had remained in town, but most had married and faced the challenges of raising children.

"I lucked out and got a job at the Port Townsend pulp mill. During the two years that I worked there, I took care of my parents. Each had become very ill and needed care. First, my mother passed on, and four months later, my father passed. I was beside myself with grief, and sometimes still am.

"In my mind, I often thought of the village where I was kept captive, and I thought of Ki Nyguen. In 1978, I decided to look for her. I was sure she was married and with children. When I reached the village, she was there, caring for siblings. She was pleased to see me, and she accepted my proposal of marriage. I thought we would live in Port Townsend, but as time went by, I started a business in Vietnam and stayed there."

The flight doctor asked, "What business did you start?"

"When I was a prisoner in the tunnels, I observed how rice paper was used for many purposes. Sometimes it was placed on an open wound as gauze to stop bleeding. Sometimes it was eaten. Other times it was used for human hygiene, and sometimes it was used as kindling. I simply started a business that took rice, boiled it, mashed it, added protein powder to it, wrapped it, and sold it. The most difficult part was the wrapping, for the four-inch squares of rice paper had to stay dry. I developed sales in Russia,

France, and Mainland China. People from Ki's village were employed and paid well. Some became rich. Slowly, I became wealthy. The government permitted me to control four hundred acres near Ki's village, and on that land, I built a factory, an airplane hangar and runway and a large mansion. The rebar in the landing field was epoxy-coated to prevent rust. As roads improved, it became cheaper to deliver my product by truck within Vietnam, but I used the large plane to haul it to distant countries."

"Where will the plane go after we leave?"

"Back to Vietnam."

"How about you?"

"Oh, I never married. I mostly studied. My parents were poor. Because I was a good student, I received many scholarships. My parents also controlled a rice pond, but there was not much money to be made."

"Have you saved money?"

"Yes, as a surgeon, I am well paid. I have about 3 million invested in index funds."

"Captain to in-flight doctor."

"Yes."

"We are three hundred miles from landing. Please prepare Mr. Rowell for leaving the plane. Strap him down."

"Will do."

"Mr. Rowell, I need to dress you, shoes and all." She grabbed the trousers and other clothes and quickly dressed Mr. Rowell.

Mr. Rowell explained, "In the bureau in the bathroom is a small backpack. It contains my passport, credit card, money, and a toothbrush and toothpaste. I can wear it."

Slowly, the plane dipped down over the Strait of Juan De Fuca. They began to cross over the Salish Sea.

"Paine Field Tower to Flight Triple Zero."

"Yes, this is Triple Zero."

"Maintain direction of approach, but do an airfield flyover at three hundred feet. Then circle counterclockwise and return for landing. You will be escorted by two growlers. Within a few minutes, two Navy Boeing EA-18G electronic attack airplanes appeared, and each took up a position two hundred feet off the wings of the 747.

"Triple Zero to tower."

"Tower, here."

"Why all the escort? Why the fuss?"

"Tower back. Your plane was built here. Several hundred Boeing employees are now outside to see the flyby. The growlers have nothing better to do. All airspace has been cleared."

Some of the older employees had helped construct Triple Zero. The 747 came over at three hundred feet. When the pilot tipped the wings, the crowd cheered and waved. Then, circling back, the plane landed.

"Thank you for helping me. Good luck in Boston."

"You are welcome. Thank you for talking with me. Good luck in your hometown."

They shook hands and then turned away.

Mr. Rowell asked the driver to place the seat at a forty-five-degree angle. And then he was assisted into the SUV. They waited an hour at the Edmonds ferry. Mr. Rowell dozed off. At the Hood Canal Bridge, there was no delay. Upon approaching Port Townsend, Mr. Rowell noticed many new businesses. At the town entry on State Highway 20, he saw once more a large grove of madrona trees, and he knew he would soon smell the fumes from the pulp mill. Descending the S curve, he observed how the boatyards had expanded. He noticed box stores to his left, where part of the Kah Tai Lagoon had once been. Ahead, he saw the courthouse. They drove along Water Street into Port Townsend downtown. After parking, the driver assisted Mr. Rowell to the registration desk of the Peninsula Hotel and then helped him walk to his street-level room. Mr. Rowell registered and prepaid for a stay of three weeks. After being paid and tipped, the driver left.

After resting on top of the bed for an hour, Mr. Rowell phoned the front desk. "Please, could you call me a cab?"

"Yes, of course, just a minute."

Shortly, the phone rang. "Taxi is here."

"Thank you. Please ask the driver to come to my room to help me walk."

"I'll ask."

"Hello. I am Gil. Need an arm?"

"Yes, please."

She steadied Mr. Rowell as they walked to her car.

"Where to?"

"Please, drive by the schools, like, start with the grade school, then the junior high, and then the high school."

"Fine."

To his surprise, all the schools he had attended had been rebuilt, and two were relocated. Even so, his mind was flooded with memories. As he glanced about, he momentarily felt young again. As though he should step out of the taxi to attend class. The yesterday of long ago refreshed his mind.

To the taxi driver, he commented, "Strange school system. Very protective of the students. We attended to learn while, at the same time, the school tried to learn about each of us. From grade to grade, a file on each student was passed along. The school probed for gifted students to draw them out. The school was on constant watch for students with neurological development issues, like dyslexia and attention deficit hyperactivity syndrome. Sometimes the school would find and attempt to treat a student who had been traumatized.

From the first grade on, music classes became more complex. At first, we sang simple songs. Then we got into folk songs. Slowly, by junior year, we were introduced to opera, and by our senior year, some students, at assemblies, actually sang operatic arias. Other classes moved from simple math to algebra, geometry to physics.

The taxi driver commented, "School was difficult for me. I dropped out. What I know I learned from talking with others."

"I understand. My grades were never good. I could not study at night and mostly disappeared out the door and walked the beaches."

"Now where?"

"Please take me to Fort Worden, to the parking lot near the lighthouse."

They entered the spacious park, passed by white-colored military dormitories that stood in a line along a flat parade ground. As the car descended a short hill, Mr. Rowell looked ahead and admired the long, curving beach. When the taxi approached the lighthouse, the driver made a sharp turn to the left, drove a short distance to a parking lot next to the beach. She positioned the car so that when Mr. Rowell lowered his window, he could look right down on the beach. Like a game of Pick-up sticks, logs lay scattered on the beach above the high-tide line. The air carried sounds of waves collapsing on the beach and then the "hiss" of the waves moving pebbles about. Farther out, canopies of kelp rose and lowered with the waves. The fronds of kelp are floating in keeping with the changing direction of the tidal current. In the distance, he observed the beige bluffs of Whidbey Island. North, he saw a faint outline of the American San Juan Islands, punctuated by the top of Mt. Constitution on Orcas Island.

"Anyplace else?"

"No, thanks, I am done. Are you from here?"

"No. I moved here four years ago. My husband is a builder of wooden boats, and he easily got a job here. I drive a cab for extra income."

At the hotel, she helped Mr. Rowell to his room. He paid her and tipped.

Again, he simply lay on top of the bed. After a while, he undressed and made his way to the bathroom and took a bath. He believed one of the joys of life was simply sitting in hot water, but he knew he could not remain too long. In about fifteen minutes, he was back on the bed.

He had saved the best for last—to walk in the darkness of the early evening to the back door of the building where he had once lived. He was about to meet his parents. Fully dressed, he left his room and began to walk along a short hallway. Suddenly, he lost his balance, and his shoulder pressed up against the wall to his right. He pushed off and kept going. A second time, he lost his balance and bumped into the wall on his left. He knew he could keep going. His parents waited. He stood on Washington Street. His legs felt weak. His body seemed top-heavy. He could not walk in a straight line. Near an antique car sales business, he turned into an alley and approached the back of the building where he had once lived. He stood before the back door, and there was no doubt in his mind that his smiling parents were on the other side, waiting to greet him.

Just next to the door, about twenty inches from the wall, rested an empty dumpster. Mr. Rowell reached for the door handle. He held it firmly and began to turn it, but just then, the excitement, his age, and the stenosis caused his heart to flutter and then stop. He stepped back and fell forward against the wall. Then he slid off to one side, where he collapsed and lay behind the dumpster.

For two weeks, as the dumpster slowly filled, no one noticed his body.

Three days after his death, room service noticed the bed had not been used and that the backpack had not been moved. After the hotel manager notified the police, a detective appeared and interviewed the taxi driver and examined the contents of the backpack.

The chaplain at the Port Townsend Veterans' Post read about the missing person in the local newspaper. His attention sharpened when he realized the missing person was a veteran and a former resident. He telephoned the post commander and then a former army buddy who presently served as commander of the Joint Base Lewis–McChord south of Tacoma.

The post members searched the beaches and the parks. A few who owned airplanes flew along the shoreline.

When the dumpster was full, it was moved, and a sanitation worker glanced back and saw the body.

About three months later, a police car and the sheriff's car pulled up to the funeral home. The officers received a cardboard shoe box containing the ashes of Mr. Rowell. As the two cars pulled away, the sirens were kept off, but the emergency overhead lights were turned on. The procession of two cars slowly passed the Hill Top Tavern and then circled down the S curve to the flats. The cars drew no attention along Water Street and made a sharp turn onto Monroe. The two cars advanced slowly over Morgan Hill and entered Fort Worden.

Upon reaching the beach, the officers were surprised to see many parked cars, trucks, and motorcycles. A man in jeans and a logger's shirt stood in the roadway and directed the officers to two reserved parking spaces.

The tide was out. The ferry could be seen making its way across Admiralty Inlet. Snow on Mt. Baker reflected the sunlight. The top of Mount Rainier could be seen through the cut. Seagulls glided about. Offshore, three pigeon guillemots kept diving and resurfacing. In the distance, a migrating loon floated, half submerged. The officers saw about thirty men and two women, all just standing about. When the officers began to walk toward the beach, the chaplain stepped forward and asked the officers to wait. Then a self-employed plumber from Quilcene stepped forward. His clothing was stained and ripped from his work underneath houses. His baseball cap was on backward. In his left hand, he held a lit cigarette.

He shouted, "Formation now! Four abreast! Front to back!" The veterans quickly shuffled about and then stood as a solid group. An electrician from the pulp mill reached into a brown-colored paper bag that had been made at the mill and pulled out a trumpet. He began to play taps, and as he was just about finished, there was heard a strange thudding, pumping, and drumming sound. The sound grew louder.

One veteran yelled, "Slicks!"

Just then, three army transport helicopters, Hueys, came over the forested hill and descended to pass over the beach at fifty feet elevation. As the helicopters passed and began to gain elevation and to circle, the outer two helicopters lowered ropes that pulled fluttering large American flags. From the third helicopter, a flag was let down. It was colored red, and in the middle was a five-point yellow star.

"My god," one vet exclaimed. "That is the flag of Vietnam."

Another veteran commented, "Maybe, just maybe, the war is over."

As the helicopters pulled away and began the long flight to the Lewis–Lewis-McChord Army base, the officers walked to the tideline and gently emptied the shoebox. Then the plumber yelled, "Dismissed," and the veterans broke rank, stood about, and left.

Three months later, the American ambassador stood before the president of Vietnam. "Your Excellency, thank you for this meeting. I am here for an unusual reason. As you may know, a Mr. Dexter Rowell lived many years in your country. Now he has passed on. I am here to read to you his last will and testament." The ambassador reached into his briefcase and pulled out a document that was encased in blue-colored parchment.

I, Dexter Rowell, a citizen of the United States of America, a single man with no living children, being of sound mind and fully alert to my circumstances, do by this, my last Will and Testament, give, devise and bequeath all that I own to the people of Vietnam.

The document was properly signed and attested to in compliance with the laws of Washington State and the rules of Vietnam.

When the ambassador stepped forward to hand over the document, he stopped because he noticed that a piece of paper had fallen from the back page of the will. Flustered, he bent down and picked up the paper, glanced at it, then decided to read it.

"I should like to add to my Will information that might otherwise remain unknown. The airfield at my home has a cement runway that is very stout. Inside the cement, the rebar is closely spaced. Each piece is epoxy-coated to prevent rust. What I wish to report is that the entire runway covers military tunnels that served as regional headquarters. The tunnels included office rooms, workshops, a hospital with a surgery room, and sleeping and cooking quarters for over 5,000 soldiers.

On the runway, here and there, are ten-inch square holes covered with a thick, coated stainless steel grill. These holes admitted oxygen to enhance the quality of the air in the tunnels. All tunnel entries are sealed except one. The one tunnel entry is at the basement of my home at the west wall, behind a locked, thick, steel door. The key to the door is taped to this paper.

Often, I think of the men, women, and children who scraped and dug the tunnels and the soldiers who lived for many years underground in the darkness. They all worked and lived bravely. I wish all the people of Vietnam well. Goodbye."